ISBN:979-8-218-10909-7

Library of Congress Control Number: 2022921885

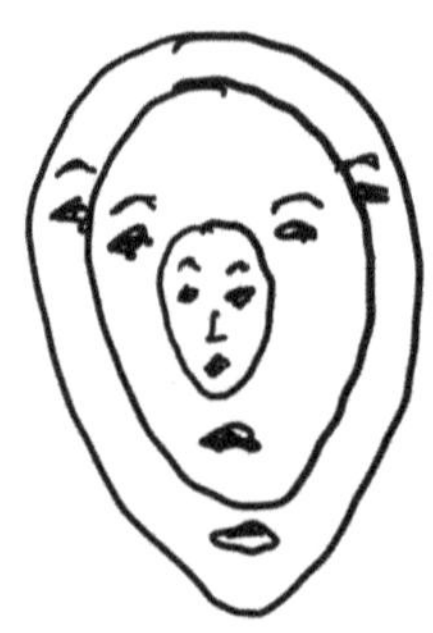

FUNNY/SAD

Written and designed
by Elena Karaytcheva

Edited by Eileen Myles

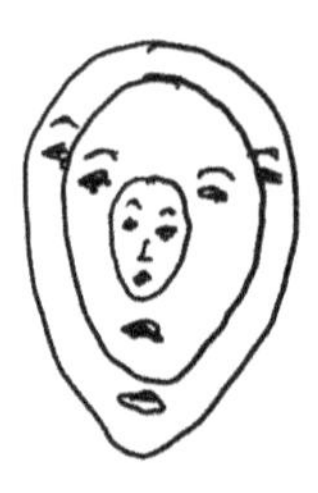

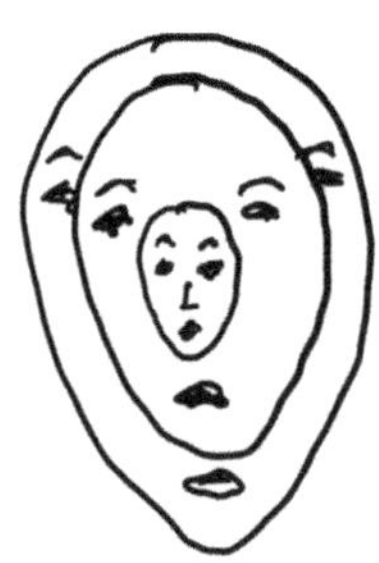

hello!

MY NAME IS ELENAKARAYTCHEVA AND I'M GOING TO BE A ~~STAR~~! THANKS FOR PICKING THIS UP. I WROTE IT VERY WELL AND I HOPE IT LANDS IN THE LAPS OF SOME OF MY FAVORITE PEOPLE IN THE WORLD. ONE DOWN... BAJILLIONS MORE TO GO. THIS BOOK IS AN ODE TO SURVIVING THE CHAOS IN YOUR MIND WHEN TRIGGERED BY MATTERS OF THE HEART. WHEN YOU LOOK BACK AND WONDER IF THAT WAS EVEN YOU? IF ANY OF THIS IS EVEN REAL? TREAD LIGHTLY. I LOVE YOU. EVK

(march 4)

This morning I peeled a hard-boiled egg over the trash can and it slipped out of my fingers and ricocheted down the liner sticking at the sides. I decided that today I will gaslight the customers that come into the shop. Not because I am cruel, but because I want to listen to the same song over and over again. If they ask me if the same song keeps replaying, I'll say no. A part of me wants to scare them into thinking they are losing their minds, too.

no. I no. I no. I n

I feel bad about that and lately for lunch I've been eating a big bowl of thinly sliced cucumbers drenched in a mixture of salt, pepper, and lime. A Rastafarian woman on Youtube told me this would make me happier in the summertime. I had sex a few days ago with someone very kind and accommodating. I felt very suspicious and today am realizing how sad it is that kindness stuns me into suspicion.

As a result, I'm going to start assuming that every man I find attractive is gay.

After work I'll chop up an onion and crunch it with salt in my hands then eat it. Yes. This way, I stay in instead of getting into trouble. It's easy with hard-boiled eggs because you're full enough to drink without getting sleepy or fat. I wash the onion down with a Sapporo and light a joint to further render myself unfit for public consumption. I've never wanted to be consumed by the public…just loved, adored, admired etc.

Today I counted the amount of times I used the word "i" in a sentence and then I stopped because it made me uncomfortable. The shittier part is that I started noticing when everyone else did it and am now convinced this society breeds narcissists. I don't want to put that out there though, and maybe if I keep it to myself they won't feel seen or justified to continue.

1.4

I prefer to hide under the covers with my warm breath instead. I feel very beautiful under here. I wonder if I should masturbate and I sort of start to but my fingers smell like latex a little and I'm reminded again that lovers can be kind and how I'm not entirely aware of that. Then I start craving a hard-boiled egg so I press on my eyeballs really hard until I see colors and shapes.

THE ONLY WAY
TO FALL ASLEEP
NOWADAYS IS
WITH
UNEVENTFUL
ASTROLOGICAL
PHENOMENA
AND A REALLY
BORING BOOK,
ANYWAY.

1.6 (fin)

no. 2 (march 5)

I've been eating a lot of expired food lately, but I've never had an eating disorder before. Not a real one. I will keep an open can of Sapporo on my bedside table when I am getting sober, though. I always thought you were supposed to lose your mind, or - I, mine. I couldn't imagine that having one that makes you feel bad was the perfect match. And then the woo's talk about shedding.

In the end, writing is the only thing that keeps me breathing in this shit-hole of an experience. The other day my boss's 17-year-old daughter told me I was so pretty and I told her that it was a mask and underneath it she'd find a gremlin. She laughed and so did I… all the way to the bank! I've never been ugly a day in my life.

My therapist tried doing a mirror exercise with me and she told me to look at my face so I did. It wasn't until she told me to look deeply into my own eyes that I got on my hands and knees and licked her hand and then crawled away barking like a dog-baby.

The idea behind the can of beer is that I can take a sip if I really want some which won't be until day two or three and it'll be warm and flat by then and it won't pinch the back of my throat the way I need it to.

2.2 (fin)

no.3 (march 6)

I check the time on my Tissot now since I've grey-scaled my iPhone. It is as boring and un-stimulating as they say. The proverbial they. I know I'm taking life too seriously when I use words like Tissot and proverbial or look at a small, purple flower blossoming from the cracks of dry, desolate land that surrounds me and don't smile.

That's typically when I'll roll a joint from a jar of weed and mix it with a little bag of flowers I keep in my kitchen.

That can't happen right now though because I've just told you that I am detoxing.

I was also never
good at math.

IT TAKES ME LONGER
than most to tell time

That she's one cold
hard bitch.

Instead, I
take naps even
when I'm not
tired because
dreaming is
more exciting
than being
awake right
now. Or
something like
that. I went
to war on my
kitchen floor.
I woke up to a
colony of ants
planning an
overthrow. I
felt very calm
except I
hadn't eaten
in awhile so
my body grew
heavy.

Not to joke
about war or
whatever, but
who else can
say they've
paused battle
for ramen
noodles? I
lied to you,
it was *No*
Chicken Noodle
soup. Salty,
yes. Instead
of chicken
they used
something else
that was chewy
and it made me
think about
how I used to
love lying.

It feels
good to say
something
better
than what
really is.

3.3

But apparently that’s a problem for people so I’ve cut back. I was always a kid with ideas. One time I was a vampire for a few months and it was a lot of fun. I believed it until other people told me it wasn’t true. It’s sad when kids try to grow up too fast. It’s creepy when kids try to get other kids to grow up too fast. I’d like to be a vampire again sometime. But not on Halloween.

3.4 (fin)

no. 4

A MAN
(april 10)
WHO USED TO PAY MY BAR TABS

AND STICK HIS MIDDLE FINGER

up my ass in the front seat of his car started watching my Instagram stories again. I passed really beautiful trash on a back road. I was listening to Jenny Hval. It was a plump, clear bag filled with lots of Chinet in it, I'm assuming.

I told someone the other night my favorite color was purple despite not seeing it much. Today, I found it in Rothko.

THE DARKNESS WILL SWALLOW YOU.

I also found it in the earrings of a self-conscious woman at the bar at 2pm. She won't alert the sommelier that she's made her choice on which white wine. The smaller flute or bigger. I'm drunk. I try to avoid places with somms because of the strange trouble it brings me.

A man at the end of the bar gifted me two bottles of wine because I smiled at him. Rather than advertising it, I thank him and then leave to smoke a cigarette. I don't care that the guy I love doesn't love me back. I get off on disappointing people.

I watch a gay man try earning his seat as the "gay friend" of some bitches in a corner.

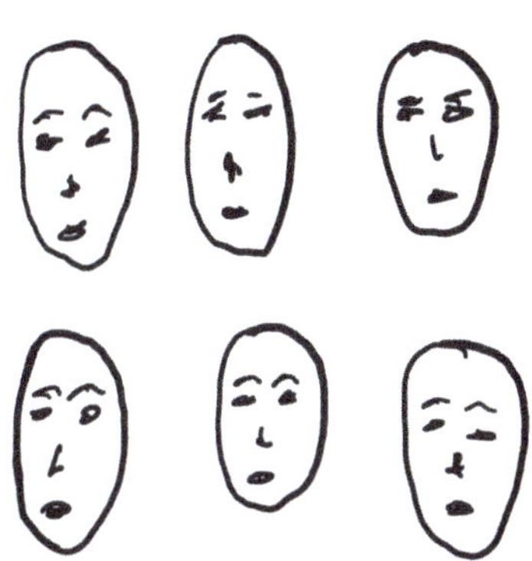

The bartender keeps calling himself a hick. Callin'. I never would've guessed if he hadn't told me. For the record. For the record. For the record.

4.4 (fin)

(may I2)

no. 5

This summer I am the
queen of the wasps.

I wake up to 3 fresh ones flying around my bedroom each morning. I like to tell them things like, “Hello” and “I love you.”

Throughout the day I’ll capture them and any newcomers using a hot pink cup and a piece of paper with Thic Nhat Han’s “Call Me By My True Names” poem printed on it. I kiss the cup and slide open my back door to set them free.

At first they're confused and angry with me. I used to think it's because they want to stay with me but that's unnatural.

Wasps just don't like to be caged, that's all. They're as unruly as I'd like to be.

Any fallen that I find in my home I memorialize.

MY MIND

HINKS IT'S

RANGE THE

AY I KEEP

EAD BUGS

AROUND.

WAY I KEEP

DEAD BUGS

AROUND.

MY MIND

THINKS IT'S

STRANGE THE

WAY I KEEP

DEAD BUGS

AROUND.

MY MIND

THINKS IT'S

STRANGE THE

WAY I KEEP

DEAD BUGS

AROUND. 5.4

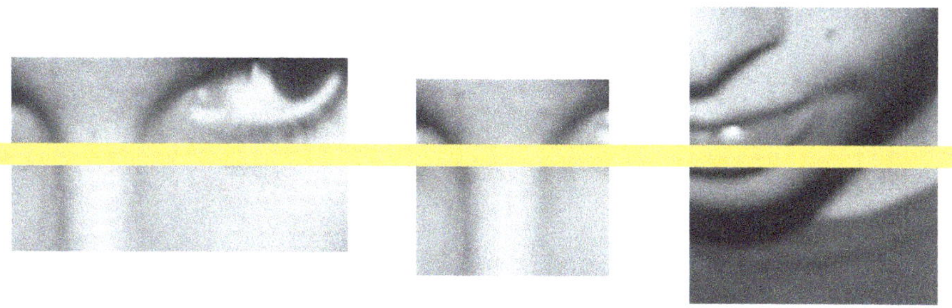

I have two laying side by side like lovers in the cap of an old candle on my kitchen counter. On extra windy days when I open my door, the wind blows them closer together. I thought maybe their family could come and visit them. I also thought that maybe I could love again, too.

5.5 (fin)

no. 6
no. 6
no. 6

GOOD APPLES GET EATEN BY PIGS

•••

(may 20)

I flicked off one of GOD's creations today, a handful of times. Then I started thinking about the people I need to stick around for. I counted them and the amount of times I've cried in the barn. To a ladybug, a bleeding arm, disbelief. Why is the number one asked question, "How are you?" Gag reflex it. I'm great. I'm good. I'm OK. I'm not bad. I have zero complaints. I'm thinking. I'm thinking about time.

6.1

I’m thinking about how much time I have left. Sorry. I’m sorry. Hey I’m sorry. I’m sorry about how I feel. I’m sorry about how I feel when there are people starving to death. I apologize to you that there’s a pit in my stomach and it wakes me up in the middle of the night asking if it’s time to open me up and swallow me whole. They say the stomach is a second brain.

6.2

I satiate my hunger with irreverence; belligerence ala carte. And really good fucking apples!

Please call me.

6.3 (fin)

no.7
(may 22)

I tried to
convince my
therapist that
the amount I
drink is not a
problem.

Society has put
these limitations
on what an
appropriate
amount of
drinking is and
that's why
everyone else is
stupid and boring
and works desk
jobs and goes on

vacation once a year. They don't fly off the handle enough to wake themselves up from the bullshit lie of a life they've been living. And as a result, they also don't make out with strangers enough. Or build tough enough skin by having to wake up early for work regardless of how hungover they are. Then she told me to call my sponsor after our session and

tell them the
same thing. I did
and they laughed
and told me they
understood, but
the beauty of
sobriety doesn't
lie in the
sobriety of
society. It lies

in the sobriety
of a recovered
alcoholic. I do
like beauty more
than drinking. I
also have a new
therapist and I
think that's fun
too. Fun fun fun

fun fun fun fun

fun fun fun fun

fun fun.

7.7 (fin)

no. 988

(june 5)

I'm gonna I'm gonna I'm gonna. Fucking snort an Adderall. Fucking fuck my crazy ex-boyfriend. Fucking rip my fucking computer in half. Fucking tape my eyeballs open at 4pm so I don't nap but I cry instead.

chless.
do it
lready.
nless.
st cum
ready.
.
m
.

there

is!

somethin

g wrong.

Fucking masturbate until
Bruise the forehead that
I get a fucking UTI.
meets the mirror. Ocean
Fucking try not to kill
taught me that a word can
myself. Look up at the
stretch a light year. Can
fucking sky and hope I
you give me one of those?
take fucking flight.
One last one, before I go?

Spread those wings, baby.

ck stop
uck stop
that.
that.

Spread em'.
for me for

me.

watch your
your step. ffollow
step. me

with you
listen
listen
listen
to me

me
over

here

8.1

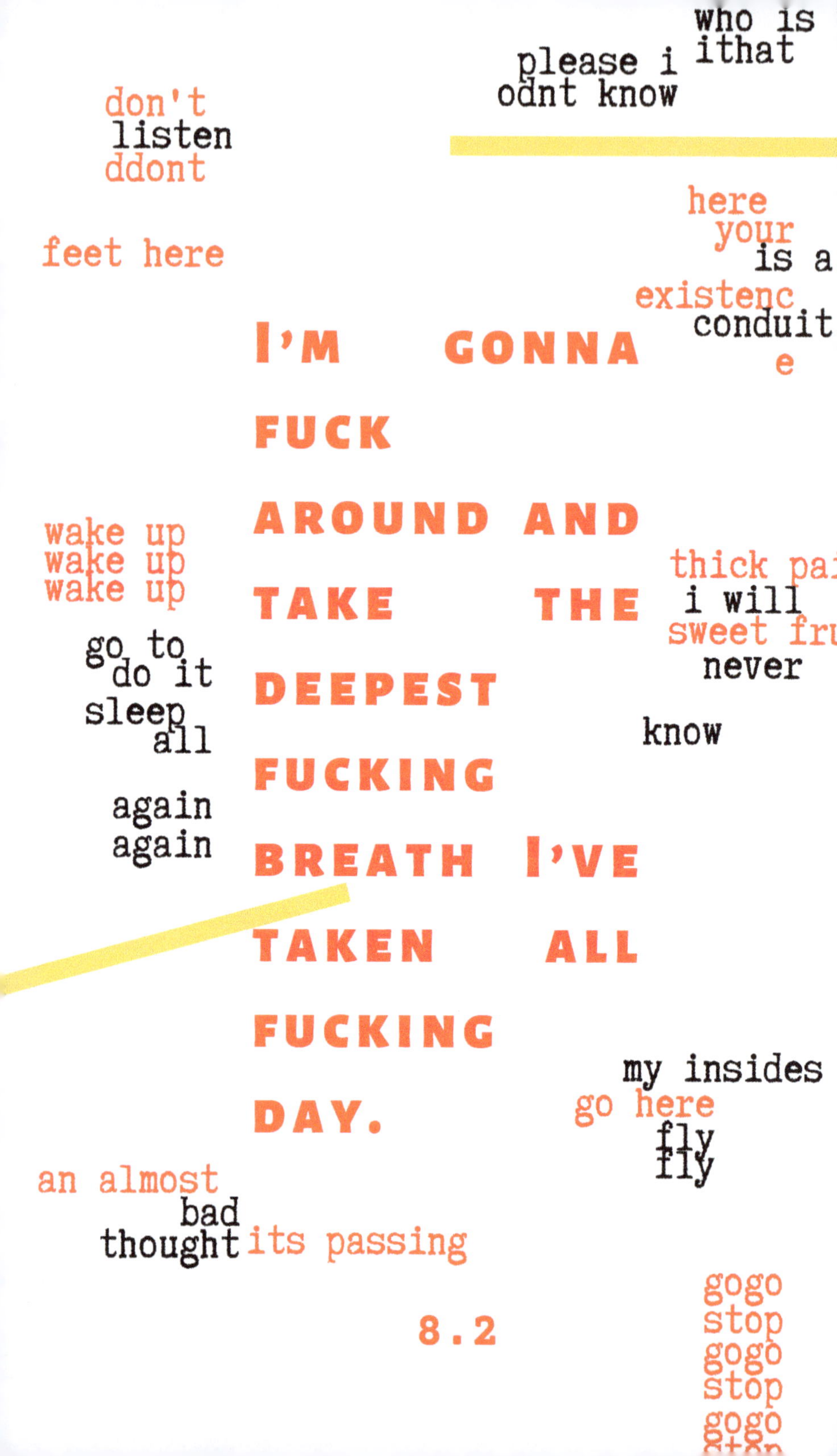
who is
ithat
please i
odnt know
don't
listen
ddont
feet here
here
your
is a
existenc
conduit
e
I'M GONNA
FUCK
AROUND AND
TAKE THE
DEEPEST
FUCKING
BREATH I'VE
TAKEN ALL
FUCKING
DAY.
wake up
wake up
wake up
go to
do it
sleep
all
again
again
thick pai
i will
sweet fru
never
know
my insides
go here
fly
fly
an almost
bad
thought
its passing
8.2
gogo
stop
gogo
stop
gogo

i i

i

i

Fucking appreciate the fucking life I've gotten to live thus far. I'm gonna fucking tell my i mom I fucking love her. Take i the fucking trash out of my fucking house. Fucking forgive the guy who broke my fucking heart. Fucking tell my friends that I'm sorry but this doesn't feel right and I need a fucking break. i Fucking keep reading books because I'm actually starting to fucking like them thank fuck.

i

i

i

i

FUCKING DRINK A SHIT GREEN JUICE FILLED WITH FUCKING NUTRIENTS. AND THEN EAT A FUCKING CHOCOLATE BAR.

THEN I'LL FUCKING TAKE A SHOWER AND BRUSH THE KNOTS OUT OF MY FUCKING HAIR.

i

i

i

i

i

I'm gonna clean my fucking car. I'm gonna drop off a surprise gift at a stranger's fucking house. And fucking tell them to keep going. And pray to fuck they don't get freaked out. I'm gonna fucking freak the fuck out. In the coolest fucking way. I'm gonna take the freak out I'm having right now and turn it into beautiful fucking art.

FUCK YOU.

8.5 (fin)

hey!

I'M ALMOST DONE! THIS IS ALMOST FINISHED! I FEEL NAUSEATED BY THE THOUGHT. AND THE REALLY STRONG COFFEE I JUST CHUGGED. I'M HAVING TROUBLE GETTING THROUGH THIS. THE MATERIAL TOOK QUITE THE TURN, DIDN'T IT? I HOPE YOU'RE TAKING DEEP BREATHS. WE'VE GOT A FEW MORE MOMENTS HERE TOGETHER. WANNA HOLD HANDS? MY BRAIN IS MELTING. LET'S DO THIS.

no.9
(june 24)

I don’t enjoy Joy Division
but I always saw the T-shirt
and thought they must be very
cool. I’m more into
entertainment via absurdity.

I haven't stretched
in weeks.

I look up to God and tell him "last one" as I open another tarot reading on Youtube.

I feel that I anticipate people's needs before they do and I cry about it curled up in a ball on my kitchen floor.

I'm better at pretending that nothing is true and life is groovy. Because it is. And because I am.

The only thing that informs my days now is self-discipline and naps.

I used to be good
at giving it up.

Now I wash my dishes everyday and sweep my floor in silence. Limited distraction helps me practice my interviews for when I'm **rich** and **famous**.

I love my dad. I think he's the wildest man I've ever met. I hope God has a beautiful place for him.

I saw a dead kitten in an old air duct this morning and threw up on my landlord's driveway.

People who can’t

control their tongue on

drugs are very

disappointing to me.

9.4 (fin)

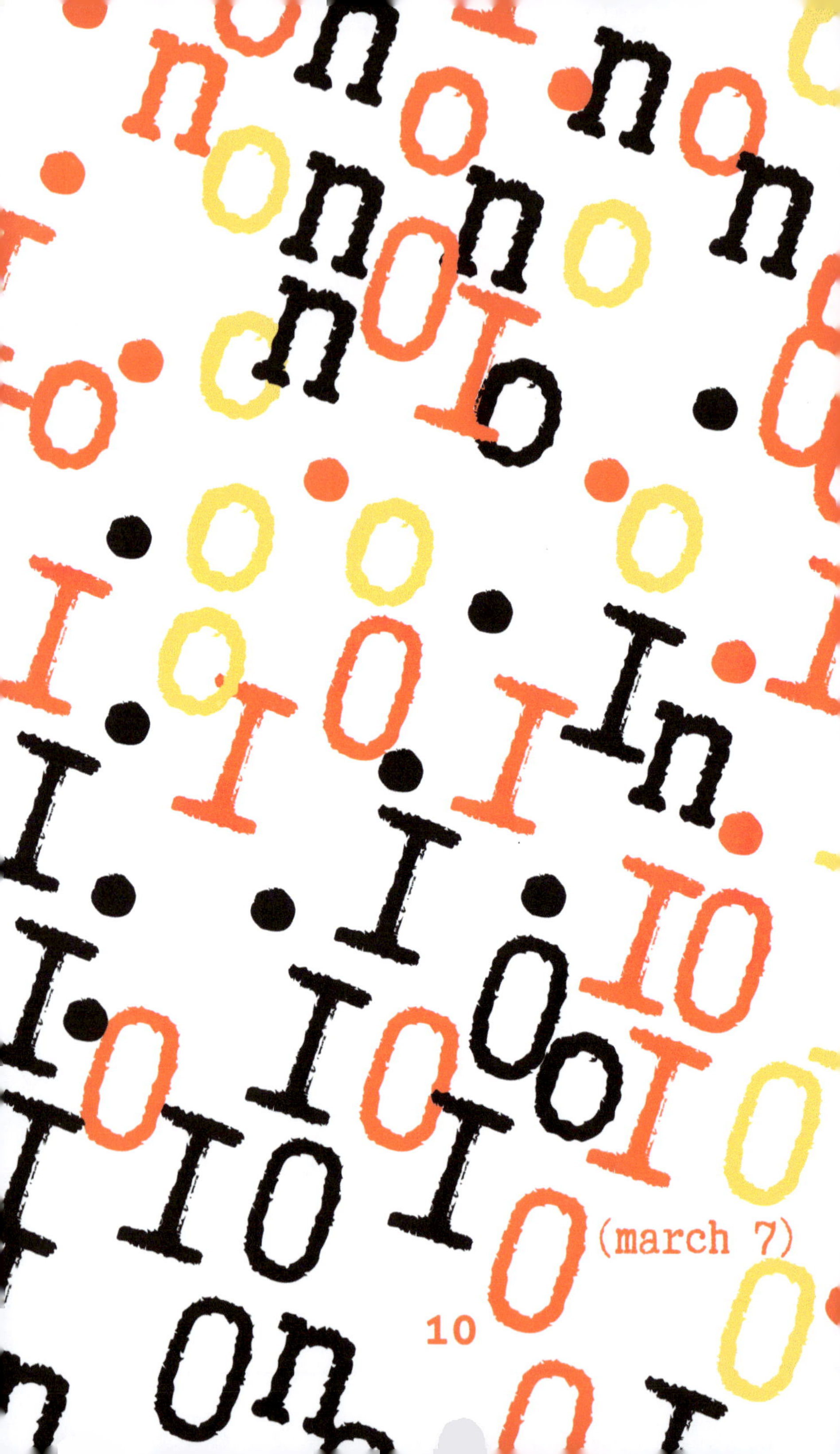
(march 7)

Dull razor blades are good. Fresh ones cause the hair to grow back sharper. With dull ones, they trim the hair and miss a few causing it to just remain kept and kind of soft in a way I can't explain. I can get behind wanting a sharper blade, though. It objectively does a better job. If I could place my knees on the cold tile of a bathroom floor and my lips on the warm blood leaking from a sad person's skin I would.

10.1

What makes clean hands happy hands? Clean skin screaming to be shed can only keep up appearances for so long. I worry about having tattoos. What if instead of being buried with them I rip them off instead? My face is a blur when I look in the mirror. To be insane I think is easier than being sane. It's my mission to be groundbreaking. I'll only self-medicate in times of desperation, though.

10.2

It feels similar to those moments in life when you want your usual overpriced latte but you have to check your bank account in the parking lot. And then you transfer from whatever obscure side wallet app you use to squirrel fund in times of need. In this case, it pays to be the sharper blade. I consider it bold to walk the same fine lines as the nouveau riche. As long as you can look at yourself in the mirror and laugh about it with partially hairy legs.

10.3 (fin)

no.II

(july I4)

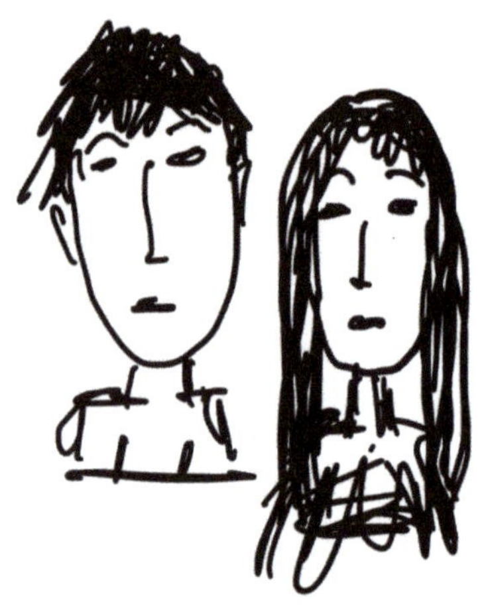

I'm weary of good looking people. They need one thing that humbles them.

Keeps them self-conscious. A flat foot or a chipped tooth. I started getting nervous about our love when he told me to shut the fuck up. And when he got so shit-faced he didn't care if his car went missing. I just wanted to know if he also feared insignificance right before closing his eyes. To love someone who hates feeling things that challenge the heart is heartbreaking.

That was when I started pressing on my eyeballs so hard they saw stars. “Are you sure this mission is still mine?” I ask the sky. I squish red berries in my hand instead of eating them because they look like sweet blood sweating out of my skin. I do this alone in my kitchen. What other choice do I have? I was beautiful to a man subscribed to an existence that on the surface is breathing, but lives in the muck. I am old enough to know better now.

11.2 (fin)

no.12

(july 20)

I always wear white on days it rains. Today I set up my voicemail greeting and made sure it had many components of my personality including my... laugh.

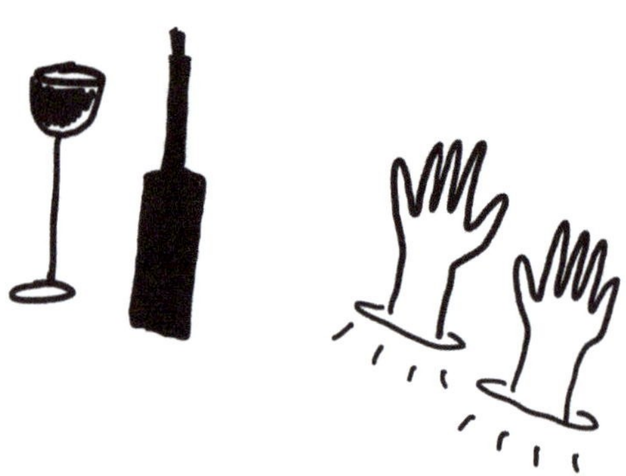

I call it consequential fantasy. Some days I feel deeply good and others I feel un-good.

12.1

It's just me and an old white guy in the laundromat. He keeps staring at me like he wants to fuck me. And I keep fantasizing that he forces me into the bathroom against my will and while we're making out I knife him to death.

THERE'S SOMETHING WEIRD IN THE AIR.

Someone told me our town has been poisoning the water with something that keeps us here.

I think it's true and it also makes me feel safe because I can blame it on something else.

CONSEQUENTIAL FANTASY.

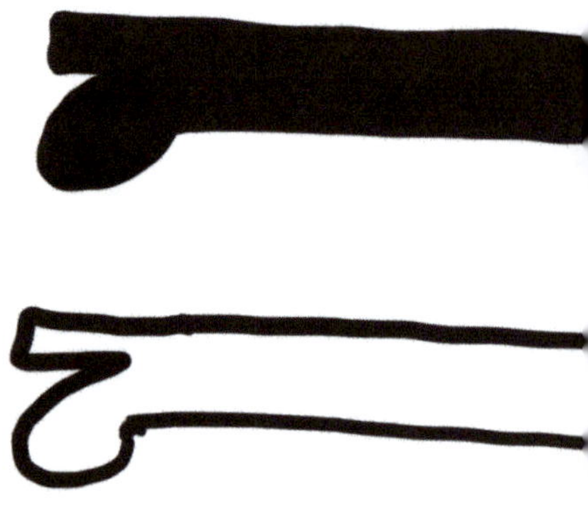

12.3 (fin)

I play games

on

the backs of

cereal boxes

no.I3
(feb 2I)

instead of doing

more important
things.

At least I did, before he
stopp,ed calling.

There's a sort of trauma involved with living in a tourist town that the locals don't talk about.

We are an island of misfit toys in the purgatory of Neverland. I thought he was my ticket out. The puzzle piece to a math equation that short-circuited long ago.

I regret not having recovered in time to have been able to let him kiss me more. Maybe then, he would've stuck around.

13.1

Today my therapist said I am dramatically codependent. Not that I am dramatic, but that my codependency goes deeper than the average.

I made a joke asking, “the average what?” I try not to hurt feelings to the point where I don’t allow people to be adults and cope with the reality of discomfort.

I should really learn to live in the moment rather than anticipate the future with an anxiety that gives me diarrhea, sometimes.

13.2 (the end)

t h a n k y o u

This work/life, wouldn't be complete without a thank you to all it's contributors; direct and indirect. I want to thank my friends and family for giving me space to be myself. It's not an easy thing to do, but I'm learning it can be when true love is present. Thank you to those who read and contributed thoughts, encouragement and some much needed humor. Fuck you but also thank you to those who brought the dark parts out. And thank you to the reader for witnessing me get butt ass naked to make something beautiful with it. Let's do it again sometime. elk♡

Please enjoy this colorfully twisted flick I made with colorfully twisted people in support of this book. “GOOD APPLES”

for u...

www.ingramcontent.com/pod-product-compliance
Lightning Source LLC
LaVergne TN
LVHW052356100826
845147LV00013B/857

* 9 7 9 8 2 1 8 1 0 9 0 9 7 *